Originally published as *Een beste vriend voor beer*
in Belgium and the Netherlands by Clavis Uitgeverij, 2019
English translation from the Dutch by Clavis Publishing Inc., New York

Visit us on the Web at www.clavis-publishing.com.

A Best Friend for Bear written and illustrated by Sam Loman

ISBN 978-1-60537-630-1

This book was printed in November 2020 at Nikara,
M. R. Štefánika 858/25, 963 01 Krupina, Slovakia.

First Edition
10 9 8 7 6 5 4 3 2 1

A Best Friend for Bear

Sam Loman

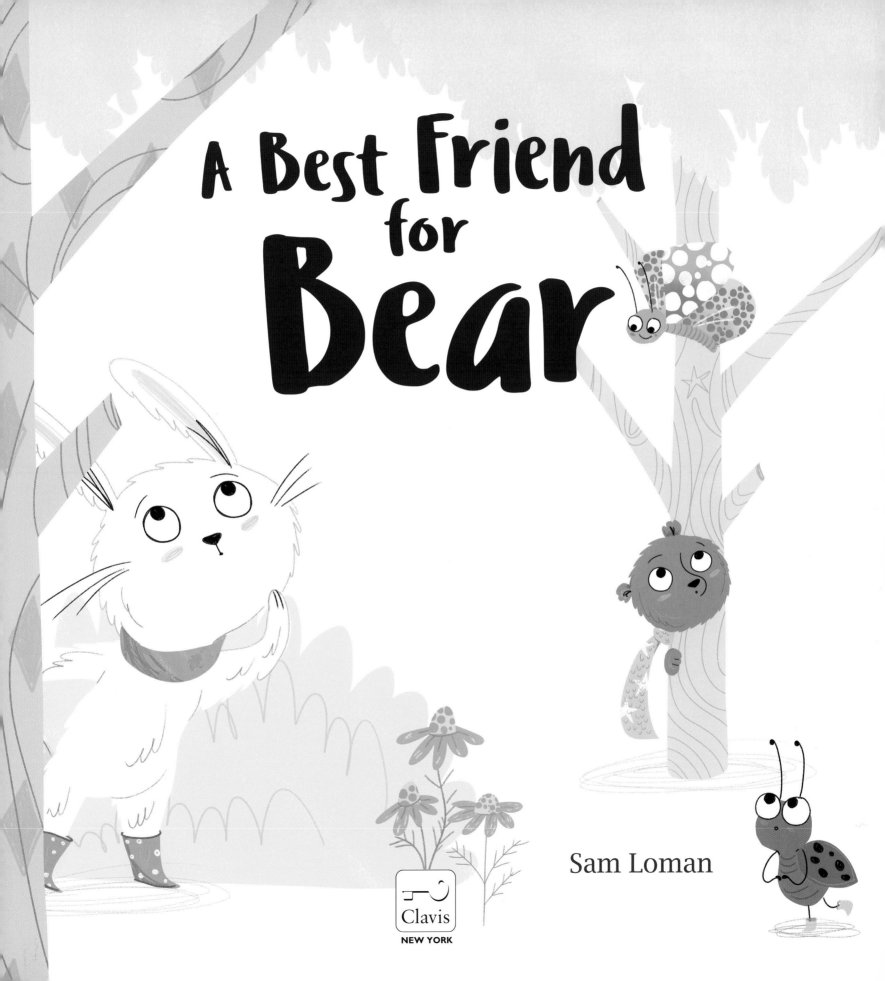

Clavis
NEW YORK

"Why do you look so sad?" asks Daddy.
"I want **a best friend** to play with," cries Bear.

"Go outside," says Daddy.
"You'll meet a friend
to play with."

Daddy and Bear look for a nice game.
What toy would **a best friend** like to play with?
A ball, a train, a scooter, a kite?
Bear chooses the ball. They can throw it to each other.

Bear wraps a scarf around his neck.
"Bye!" he tells Daddy.
He runs outside.

Bear walks with his ball deep into the forest.
Will he meet **a best friend** over there?

Bear searches behind the trees,
between the bushes, and under the rocks . . .
But he only finds a ladybug and a snail.

They're too small
to play with the ball!

"Are you looking for something?" a voice says. It's **Rabbit**.
Bear answers: "I'm looking for **a best friend**. Will you help me?"

Rabbit searches . . .

"Sorry, I can't find a best friend."

Owl flies down to them.
"What are you doing?" he asks.

"Bear is looking for **a best friend**," says Rabbit.
"Do you know where we can find one?"

Owl flies to the highest branch in the tallest tree.
He looks all around. "Nothing here!" he calls out.
"I only see Fox. Maybe she can help you."

"Where are you going?" asks **Squirrel**.
"To Fox," says Bear. "She knows where
I can find **a best friend**."
"Oh, wait! I'll come with you!" says Squirrel.

"Why are you rushing?" asks **Badger**.
"We're going to see Fox," Squirrel explains out of breath.
"She knows where Bear can find **a best friend**."
"Oh, I'll come along!" says Badger.

"How nice of you to come to my house," says **Fox**. "We're on a mission," explains Badger. "Owl told us you know where Bear can find **a best friend**."

Fox shakes her head.
"I think that Owl has it wrong," she says.
"Oh." Bear is sad.

Bear sits on a rock. "Maybe I should play
with the ball by myself," he sighs.
Then he feels something on his shoulder.

It's the warm, soft hand of Squirrel.
"You're not alone," she says. "I'm here . . .
and Rabbit, Owl, Badger, and Fox are here too."

It's quiet for a moment.
Then Bear says: "I think that
I found **a best friend** after all.
Actually, I found five best friends!"

"You're my best friends!" Bear says happily.
"Shall we play with the ball together?"